THE LADIES
OF
NEW SALEM

ANGEL COX

THE LADIES
OF
NEW SALEM

ANGEL COX

The Ladies of New Salem
Angel Cox

Book design and layout by HerEthics Books

Angel Cox asserts the moral right to be identified as an author of this work.

This book is a work of fiction, names, characters, businesses, organizations, places, events and incidents are the product of the author's imagination. Any resemblance to actual persons, living or dead, events or locations is entirely coincidental.

CreateSpace, Charleston SC
ISBN -13: 9781499507287

"Crux sacrasit mihi lux/ no draco sit mihi dux
Vade retro satana/ numquam suade mihi vana
Sunt mala quae libas/ Ipse venema bibas"

> *"Let the Holy Cross be my light/ let not the dragon be my guide*
> *Step back, Satan/ never tempt me with vain things*
> *What you offer me is evil/ you drink the poison yourself."*

CONTENTS

PROLOGUE   *I*

PART I   **1**

1 CHAPTER ONE   3

2 CHAPTER TWO   7

3 CHAPTER THREE   9

4 CHAPTER FOUR   13

5 CHAPTER FIVE   15

6 CHAPTER SIX   19

7 CHAPTER SEVEN   21

8 CHAPTER EIGHT   25

9 CHAPTER NINE   29

10 CHAPTER TEN   33

PART II   **37**

11 CHAPTER ELEVEN   39

12 CHAPTER TWELVE   43

13 CHAPTER THIRTEEN   47

14 CHAPTER FOURTEEN   49

Prologue

Deep in the swamp through the trees hung with lace
In the light of the moon showing their moves of grace
Swayed the ones in black with a white, hissing snake
Whispering the name of the soul they were about to take.

The year 1743- on the ship The St. Ursin bound for America

A young woman sat in the black bowels of the ship. Only the dusty shafts of sun punched through the wooden slats above to break the darkness. Her slender, bronze ankles were loosely bound. The men had been given direct orders to not flaw her skin in any way.

She was to be delivered to her owner, Henry Roche Belaire, in perfect condition. They kidnapped her in the middle of the night from her home in Senegal. The new master waited for her in New Orleans. Marguerite was a slave.

She sat in a puddle of saltwater and urine, still wearing the thin nightdress. Frightened beyond belief, she held tight to the only thing she managed to bring with her, an amulet. While being transported to the ship, Marguerite slipped the amulet from around her neck and wound it in the back of her thick, black hair. It was a simple amulet, strung onto a piece of old leather. Carved out of wood in the shape of a circle, it had a small, orange stone embedded at the top.

It was given to her by a very powerful Mambo back home; someplace she would never see again. The amulet gave her personal strength, and she squeezed it as she whispered prayers to God and incantations to the Mawu.

Sept. 10, 1801 - New Orleans, LA

Even still smeared with her mother's blood, the baby was beautiful. Her black hair and smooth, yellow skin promised that the beauty of her great-grandmother had been passed down yet another generation. Father Antonio de Sedalla was present at the birth upon the request of Marguerite d'Arcantrel, the mother of the child. She was a devout Catholic, attending mass every day until a few weeks before the birth. Marguerite, like her mother and grandmother, had learned the griots of vodun, and had intertwined this rich heritage into her fierce faith in God.

The smell of sweet anise seed burning in the room was a sign of this heritage, believing to bring strong powers to the baby being brought into the strange and mysterious world of New Orleans. Father Antonio placed his hand upon her small forehead and blessed her Maurie Catherine Laveau. Then he took out a small silver cross on a delicate chain and placed it around the baby's neck.

Maurie was born the illegitimate child of Marguerite d'Archantrel and Charles Laveaux. She was a creole, a free woman of mixed race. Her grandmother bought her own freedom in 1795, and purchased a small cottage on Saint Ann's Street in 1798 where they resided at her birth. Maurie's mother was the concubine of Henri D'Arcantrel, but had an affair and bore Maurie by Charles Laveaux, a mulatto man. Maurie inherited the house and lived there until her death.

PART I

Chapter One

A waft of perfume-infused smoke snaked its way out of the beaded door; a mix of licorice and wood with a hint of rosemary. The air outside was hot and muggy, yet all windows were closed and the drapes were drawn. Twirling softly, an antique ceiling fan stirred the dust particles into a swirling dance of tiny pearls in the shafts of light that squeezed through the closed drapes. A fancy woman of ivory skin stood in the front room waiting for her appointment.

Crosses, stars, triangles, weapons, animals, angels, virgins, whores, devils, numbers, and shapes of all kinds were known symbols of religion across the world. They were displayed in a variety of ways. The beads gently parted from a side door and a very small, dark woman, dressed all in white, drifted in. Her head was wrapped in a white turban. She stood there patiently as if reading the white woman's thoughts. The lady noticed the trinkets in the small one's hands; a round, blue bundle tied together with some string, a used candle, and something that looked as if it once belonged to something alive. She held them with open palms, offering them in a very subtle way.

Without sharing a word, the lady opened her hands and the small, black woman gently placed them there. Then, she turned and walked back into the beaded room. The lady followed.

The room was lit with a small, ornate ceiling light giving out a small glow, and some candles placed here and there. But the main source of light came from a huge fireplace on the back wall. It was big enough for the small woman to stand in straight up. The outside temperature was sweltering; yet standing here in this room with a roaring fire was not uncomfortable at all. A tall, beautiful woman sat at the table in front of the fireplace.

Maurie fingered the necklace she wore, an old, worn piece of leather holding a small silver cross, and a wooden amulet. The amulet was a circle with two stones embedded in it; a small orange one at the top, and a purple one, the same size, on the right side of the circle. She was told the purple stone, added by her mother, gave spirituality and psychic power to its wearer. The amulet came with her great-grandmother from Senegal, and the cross was given to her by Father Antonio on the day of her birth. She smiled slightly and offered the chair opposite her at the table.

Wealthy women came from all over the city to Maurie Laveau's home to be pampered with massaging fingers as Maurie dressed their hair with oils, perfumes, and hot treatments that make it shine and bounce. She knew ways to change the drab color of their hair to beautiful golden browns or fiery reds. It was if by magic she could transform them into beautiful women that looked younger than they were. They also came for other things, and this back room was well-known to them as well.

Politicians, wives of politicians, the wealthy and the not-so-wealthy, whites, blacks, mixed races, priests, preachers, even scoundrels and thieves came to Maurie Laveau's home for her advice, potions, and hexes that were sought after in New Orleans. Crystals, dolls, incense, herbs, cards, gris gris; they were all ready for these visitors who came for healing, love, power, wealth, and evil against their enemies. Many readings and spells were performed in this back room where this lovely lady sat. Most people were afraid of her power, but they didn't hesitate to ask for her help. It was frightening to the rich and powerful the many things Maurie knew of their secret lives. She revealed their lovers, enemies, fears, and sins. When it came to power in New Orleans, no one had more that Maurie Laveau. But the swamps held a different story.

The woman sat stiffly in the chair opposite the beautiful lady. Maurie didn't speak, but looked at her very much like the small, black woman had earlier, as if reading her thoughts and seeing into her soul. A tingle went down the woman's spine and she began to feel a bit uncomfortable. It was her first time to visit Ms. Laveau's home.

"I know why you have come," Maurie finally spoke. "Your husband, the counselor, is seeing another. You came to ask for harm, but I will tell you now that there are other ways to bring your husband back to you. The fault lies within you. How far are you willing to go to bring your husband's faithfulness back home?"

The astounded woman, ashamed that Maurie knew of her request, answered with wide eyes, "I do want him back, but I want him, and that woman, to pay for what they have done."

"You are not to judge others' sins when you have your own," Maurie said calmly.

The fancy lady stood up as if to leave. Her face turned pale, and she sat back down as tears started to slide down both sides of her face. How did this woman know of her infidelities? She was so careful. Her secret meetings with the finely muscled black men that her husband bought to work their sprawling plantation were masterfully carried out. No eyes saw her come or go, and their loyalty and silence had been bought with her sultry body and willingness to do things most wealthy, white women would never dream of.

The woman looked deeply into Maurie's eyes for the first time. She saw something in those dark orbs that said to listen to her wise words. She knew Maurie could ruin her, and her husband, in any minute's notice. Now, her mission was to keep this woman, and the slave men, silent. Her want for vengeance had turned to fear of exposure.

Maurie picked up the gris gris packet the small woman gave to the lady. She lit the candle and held the small packet over it. As the heat from the candle drifted up through the cloth, a smell of several herbs started to fill the room. She made an S shape from the woman's head to her belly, and blew the smell from the bag toward her.

"I cannot forgive your sins, or the sins of your husband. I also cannot send harm to his lover because of your own. I have asked for Eros to whisper to your husband and send fear for the woman and longing for his wife. This should stop his infidelities. But yours are much harder to break. Your appetite for your young men has grown strong. The gods will not look favorably on you if you try to work them only for your own good. You should confess your infidelities and put out the fires that burn inside you."

Rage crept into the lady's mixed feelings. She had come to Maurie for help, yet here she was chastising her for things she shouldn't even know.

"Je vas te passe une calotte," she muttered.

Suddenly, Maurie sat the bag ablaze and threw it into the fire. She stood up and towered over the now frightened lady, turned and walked out.

Chapter Two

The counselor stepped out of the carriage. He had struggled through a long day in court, and was feeling a strong sensation to spend a quiet evening with his wife. She was a beautiful woman, strong and well-shaped. She became his wife five years ago, and had been the perfect hostess and counselor's wife.

When they first married, she was shy and almost placid in bed. He was gentle and tried to make her feel comfortable in their lovemaking. He was not a muscular man, but had a smooth face and a wit that made her laugh, at least back then. He always felt as if he was trying too hard to please her, and this led to a wandering eye, which finally landed on a young, unmarried woman. But tonight, the reality of his affair had sent him home. He knew his wandering, if revealed, could ruin his reputation of a solid, outstanding lawyer. How could he be trusted if the people knew about his broken vows to such a lovely woman?

After a respectful greeting to his staff, he started up the wide staircase to his wife's room. She would probably be reading or working on the piece of artwork that stood by the window on an easel. They had no children. She had taken up the hobby of oil painting, and was quite good at it. Her first work was framed and hung in the library of their massive home. The colors were vivid and her use of light was amazing for a beginning artist.

He tapped lightly on the door, and then opened it to see his wife lying on the massive bed. At first, he thought she must have fallen asleep while working on the art piece. Her hands were covered in red, and it was spilling out over the soft, white feather comforter. Alarm slammed into his head as he realized that it was not paint, but blood, that was spilling out over the bedding. A bloody chicken's foot lay a few inches from his wife's lifeless hand.

The counselor put the foot in his pocket and then called for help.

Chapter Three

The sky was as dark as an underground cave. No moon showed this night. The ones that gathered in the gated field of Congo Square, just outside of the French Quarter, were anxiously awaiting her arrival. As soon as she was seen walking toward them, the drums began to beat. Candles flickered in the tepid breeze and danced to the rhythm. Maurie entered the gates and immediately stood still for a long moment. Then her body began to sway and move to the quickening beats. Somewhere, either from her flowing dress or her high headdress, a white snake appeared and began wrapping itself around the swaying woman. Dancer and snake became a twisted movement that grew wilder as the drums beat faster.

Others begin to move around, while some watched her as if in a trance. The snake unwrapped itself from Maurie and began to slither in the dirt. It moved in and out of the dancers' feet and disappeared into the darkness. Maurie and the others continued their maddening weaving and swaying until suddenly the drums went silent, and the dancers froze. Only Maurie moved in and around the others like a ghost moving among statues. No one knew when she left. She was just gone, like the snake. One by one, the people in the field moved toward the gate until the last person was gone. The sounds of the drums lingered in the night air and moved in and out of the dreams of the sleeping.

⌒⌒⌒

The next morning, as the sun shone on the streets of the Crescent City, Maurie Laveau entered the doors of St. Louis Cathedral while the bells of mass tolled loudly, calling all Catholics to its sound. She doused herself with holy water and crossed herself as she entered, moving toward her pew three rows from the front. Father Antonio smiled at his most famous patron and faithful partner in medicine. People around her stared in silent awe and recognition, and whispered gossip to each other of the tales that surrounded Maurie's presence.

October 20th, 1820 – In the swamps of South Louisiana

The wind blew the lace in the trees, swirling the ghost dancers into a frenzy in the midnight sky. The small shack glowed with candles, and the howls of a woman in labor filled the bayou.

A young black girl administered help during the birth. No sweet scents burned to cover the smell of blood and urine. A final curdling scream was cut off by the sudden cry of a baby that floated down the black waters to where the coven sat. The conjurer placed the final ingredient into the smoldering pot, and a murder of crows rose into the moonless sky.

The child was silent now. The young girl left the baby wrapped in a bloody blanket at the edge of the murky, black water of the swamp. A hooded figure came out of the darkness. It reached for the bundle, and returned into the shadows as the ghost dancers swirled and the crows followed their path.

April, 1836 – New Orleans

Christelle Bonnaire was not her real name. In the coven, where she learned everything of the dark magic that was conjured there, she was known as Rita. Her birth was planned, and her gifts were many. Her mother, a lady of the evening, had been kidnapped from the streets of the Crescent city as the child grew inside her. It was the baby they wanted.

Rita was taught by the Dark One, and the hags pampered her like their own child. Her powers grew in strength. Since her mother was mortal, Rita could not shape-shift, but the magic within her had been given on the night of her birth. Her spells and conjures were without fail. Only the Dark One had control over her.

At sixteen, Rita changed her name and left the swamp for the streets of New Orleans. As Christelle Bonnaire, it didn't take long to find a wealthy man to set her up as his concubine. With a nice, little apartment at the edge of the French quarter, she worked her way up in society circles. She caught many men's attention with her beauty, and a little help from her potions and charms. The women of the city whispered rumors behind her back, but they only made Christelle flaunt her wares even more. It was in her blood.

Her first encounter with the Voodoo Queen wasn't by chance. Maurie had heard many rumors of Christelle, and had an idea that she might be a witch. Christelle had been warned that her true identity would be jeopardized if she came too close to Maurie, but she was young, foolish, and curious.

Chapter Four

Walking home from the market, Christelle found herself on Saint Ann Street. Out of curiosity, she turned left and stopped in front of a small brick house. The windows were open and a sweet smell filled the air. Wanting to test the Queen's powers, she stood at the gate and mumbled an incantation. In less than a minute, a shadow appeared through the open window, and Christelle felt a tingle crawl up her spine. A large crow landed on the gate, sending a warning squawk at her.

Christelle turned away and walked back towards home. She had a visitor coming soon.

Maurie watched her leave. "Foolish macaque," she whispered. "One day, your crows will not be able to protect you. Your magic is powerful, but your gifts come from the dark one. I will keep you in your place."

Several large crows perched on her ridge row as she opened the iron gate. He was seated inside the parlor waiting for her return.

"Mon cher, where have you been?" he spoke in the shadows.

Looking into his eyes, she answered, "The market."

"Your truth is your lie. Madam Laveau has left you alone in your activities in her city, but you have challenged her with your pride and curiosity. Many years of wisdom and experience stand strong against your youthful foolishness. Her followers are many, and your activities have caused this city to frown upon you. Today the line was crossed, and you will always be in her eye."

Christelle walked past him, putting her packages in the back room. She knew he was gone. She said to no one, "Vieux, you know nothing of my true powers," and began to prepare oils and charms for her suitor.

Chapter Five

"She is making big mistakes. I don't think she is ready to be on her own," whispered the impish hag. She didn't usually speak her mind since all of their thoughts were known by the other. But this seemed important enough to say aloud. Only his thoughts were kept to himself.

"She is trying to find out how powerful she really is. Yes, she is young, but we cannot keep her here any longer. Don't question my plan. Most importantly, don't ever leave her alone. Others now know she is one of us. Keep her away from Maurie and her clan. She cannot be drawn by their ancient sorcery." The Dark One had said all that was needed. The Murder flew towards the city.

The front door of Maurie's home was used for clients; the back door was to leave unnoticed by them. As the front door opened for the wife of a very prominent congressman, another was leaving through the back with charms and potions in hand. The congressman's wife came to have Maurie's magic make her look younger than 52 years. Maurie made her hair flow like a teenager's and the gray she hid by stains from berries that were only found in the deep weeds of the swamp. Their dark maroon juices, mixed with oils and scents, made her hair shine with youthfulness. Maurie's magic was worth the money.

It took a few hours for Maurie to work her magic, and the congressman's wife had no problem passing that time with gossip about the prominent people of New Orleans.

"Maurie, you do know how to make a woman feel beautiful. You have magic in your hands. I was telling Madame Boudeaux just last night that she should make an appointment with you. Oh, let me tell you…there are some shocking stories I have heard about her…"

Maurie listened politely as she worked the oils and juices into her hair. All of this information had become useful to the promotion of Maurie's status. She had become the confidante of the city's wives and the holder of their secrets. It had also made her wise with useful knowledge which could be used in rituals and incantations. Maurie had no friends, but many followers.

Maurie's magic had only failed her once. The Dark One's was just too powerful that time, and a child's life was lost. Voodoo, as she practiced it, was never used to harm unless it was to save an innocent life. A child's soul was upheld higher than any other in the voodoo religion. She hated his power and feared him, too.

Every night, Maurie said prayers to Jesus Christ, and then to the Loa. On Saturday evenings the smell of absinthe and anise seed made their way on the night breeze through the streets of the city. The anise seed was used to ask for power and the absinthe conjured the dead.

She never asked for help from the demons, and refused to help those that wanted to harm others. She knew the people of the city feared her power and considered her a witch. She heard their whispers as she walked by, and could only ignore their ignorance. She knew the true witches of New Orleans, and they were not to be crossed. She only wanted to be respected and believed that her powers were true. They could save relationships and lives. They could bring rain when needed and scare away pestilence. The great Mississippi had even heard her commands. But every night, she remembered the one life that was lost, and vowed her revenge, with the help from the gods of the vodun.

Chapter Six

Christelle woke from a fitful sleep. She knew she was not alone, but could not see anyone through the hazy darkness of her room. Hissing, she moved like a cat and began her familiar incantations against the enemy. But her words felt empty as they did not lead her to where the intruder was hiding.

Then, she heard a giggle coming from behind. It sounded like a child's, and Christelle, for the first time in her life, was frightened. Twirling around, she surveyed the empty room. She lit a candle and sent a faint light into the corners to find the child. A gentle tug on her night dress twirled her again, and Christelle said aloud, "Show yourself evil one." This was only met with another distant giggle, and then it was gone.

Infuriated, Christelle ran to the window and flung it open. She looked for the damned crows that were usually perched on her sills. They were nowhere to be found. She spit into the night air and left the window open, daring the spirit to appear again.

The things she needed were found deep in the swamp. Wrapping herself in a thick cloak, Christelle made her way through the silent streets to the edge of the town. She was not afraid of the night swamp. It was her birthplace. She became part of it as she disappeared into the shadows of the cyprus trees. She heard their caws in the distance coming to find her. Walking to the water's edge, she picked different leaves and dug for roots. Christelle filled her deep pockets with them. Then she plunged her hand into the green moss on the edge of the water and felt through the sticky mud for the last thing she needed. It was smooth and fit perfectly in the palm of her hand. She held the oval above her head, and saying the words of the ancient ritual, she squeezed her hand tight and felt the shell of the egg break; the liquid inside flowed through her fingers. The powers from the tiny animal that was living inside were now hers to use. The Murder landed around her and the cackle of the witches broke the silence of the swamp.

◦◦◦

From the darkness of the trees, the little girl watched as the lady swayed in the circle of the witches. She smeared the liquid from the egg onto her face. It shone in the sliver of the moonlight that broke through the clouds. The girl stifled a giggle, knowing the conjuring was for her, but it didn't work. She was already there. And as long as Lisette's stolen soul lived inside Christelle, her magic was powerless against the child.

Chapter Seven

It had been over one hundred years since the witches were burned at Salem. The Dark One stood among the people of the town and watched silently in amazement and amusement of their own stupidity. Witchcraft and its dark magic had been around since the beginning of time, when Satan walked the earth freely and tempted Eve with the fruits of the garden. Those silly little girls were only bitches, not witches, using their lies and pranks to bring innocent people to the burning post for their own enjoyment and feeling of power. Salem was a perfect example of the ignorance of humanity and their fear of the unknown. He loved the thought that mere children could create such a frenzy of terror. It made his work so much easier.

His name, which was unknown to everyone, was Azazel. He had lived since Babylon ruled the earth. He was one of the many that fell from grace onto the earth to cause havoc and chaos throughout the time of the humans. New Orleans, with its influence of dark magic, had lured him as a challenge among those that use Christianity to influence their chants and spells. Maurie

Laveau had become an icon of Voodoo and Catholicism mixed to conjure spells that were powerful enough to get his attention.

Sixteen years ago, a child suffered a grave sickness. Another was on its way to being born. At the time of the sick child's death, Azazel stole the young child's soul, even while battling Maurie's spells to save her. It was hidden inside the new born child; soon to become the Dark One's prodigy.

Maurie knew she was up against someone with great power. He was close; she had seen the coven swarming the sky. And their appearance at Christelle Bonnaire's residence told her that this was where the stolen soul can be found. She needed to find the lost spirit to help her overpower the Dark One. But so far, her conjuring of the dead had not produced the young spirit. She was blocking her spells for some reason. Maurie had to find a way to convince her she was trying to help. Otherwise, this little one was out there all on her own; lost without a soul to continue her journey to heaven. She must be an amazingly strong spirit.

"I'll find you, Mon Cher. You won't be alone for long. Just trust your Mambo."

The Murder of crows perched upon Christelle's roof ridge awaiting the first light of the morning. Suddenly, the sinking moon was blocked from their sight as thousands of blackbirds appeared in the sky. The blackbirds swarmed the small cottage of Christelle Bonnaire as the crows tried to flee. The black cloud of birds formed a shadow of swarming chaos. The frantic caws of the crows were drowned out by the energetic chirping of the blackbirds. Christelle threw open her window to see the swarming cloud disperse into the night; caws and chirps growing distant, leaving only a slight mist across the street that resembled the disappearing shape of a small child.

"Absum vos malum phasmatis. Licentia meus presentia quod servo mihi Atrum Unus," Christelle whispered, as she felt fear for the second time in her life.

Who was this spirit taunting her? Why had the incantation not sent it away? How could the spirit of a child be stronger than the magic she just performed.

Christelle sniffed the air. She smelled scents of Anise and Absinthe. "Someone else is trying to conjure your soul, little Salope." She kept the window open. "Come see me."

Chapter Eight

The hags huddled in the shadows as Christelle lashed at The Dark One. They expected a fight, but he remained silent.

"Who is this babette that is stalking my dreams? Why can't I send her away with my spells? You know. I demand you to tell me!"

The Dark One stared at her with no expression. He was neither intimidated nor amused by her ranting. His thoughts were in finding the lost spirit. While her soul was trapped inside Christelle, she was immune to any and all of their spells. She must be ready to fight for it, and this put him in a dangerous sort. He conjured the soul, which made him the Utroque, point of revenge from both sides. If Laveau found out, she would throw in her works. He could lose his mortality from a young, soulless spirit and a Voodoo witch! Kings, and even gods, had tried to condemn him to hell. They had all lost their own souls in the battle.

In anger he pointed at Christelle. "Silentium!" he whispered with cold, evil eyes. Her words were trapped in her frozen lips. Her eyes widened. He has never cast upon her before.

Christelle turned on her heel and left. The Murder was flying in circles above her head, their caws sounded clearly of laughing hags. She looked up and one fell to the ground. The rest flew off and away from her wrath.

The small spirit heard Maurie's chants. She trusted no one and stayed clear of the fingers that were coming closer to reach out to her.

Maurie burned the absinthe and camphor to conjure the spirit and overpower The Dark One. She stood at the tomb where the child's body was laid sixteen years ago, leaving small trinkets to lure her. She knew she was wondering out there alone. She must find a way to let her know she is a friend, not an enemy, and must keep her away from Christelle.

The moon was full. Maurie lit the red candle and whispered, "The god of the dead, Mephistopheles, binds thee to me!" She called out the spirit's name three times, "Lisette, Lisette, Lisette! I have the power to help send you to the angels. Please come forth and accept my help. I held your hand when you passed. I did not take your soul. Nuvus liber animus! Hear my call and appear."

Lisette heard her. She was tired of being alone, and she did remember Maurie's soft hand holding hers as she slipped from her fevered body. She was scared of the dark streets and the strange people that now occupied her home. But could she trust her? Even in her young years, she remembered her mother speaking of the lady that sat in the front of the church every Sunday. She feared her and said she used the devil's work. But when Lisette turned sick, her mother called for Father Antonio who brought Marie to her bedside. Her mother looked worried, but trusted the Father with her own soul. After she left her body, she remembers Maurie's tears that mingled with her mother's. She seemed genuinely sad and comforted her mother the best she could. Lisette called out to her weeping mother, but no more than a wisp of a breeze was heard.

Lisette smelled the herbs and was scared of the snake that Maurie brought to her tomb. The candles made shadows dance on the bricks. The child just wanted her mother, but Maurie was the only one there. Stepping out of the darkness, Lisette smiled and Maurie and took her hand.

Christelle's anger had not ebbed. Being chastised in front of the hags had made her blood boil. The Dark One treated her like a child. She hasn't even changed out of her traveling clothes, as she gathered her goods: red candle, black candle, herbs, knife, and blood.

Lighting the red candle, Christelle sliced her palm and mixed the fresh drops of blood with the other. She sprinkled two pinches of dirt with the blood and then added a variety of herbs to the mixture.

"Mortus animus liber consurgo nuvus animus!

Addo mihi tui opes facuttas ex deus or malus peior pessimus!" she whispered over and over, dipping her fingers in the mixture and painting circles around the burning candle.

The candle flame grew tremendously, and then a cold, quick breeze blew it out completely. Christelle stared in disbelief as the smoke from the candle made a straight line into the air.

"Damn you! Damn your soul to hell!" Christelle shouted. The crows outside the windows began to caw and flew up into the night sky. A single tear slid down her cheek. It was the first time Christelle had ever felt this emotion; despair.

Chapter Nine

The red dust on Christelle's steps was an embarrassment. She was stooping to Voodoo tactics and that was below her. But, she would do anything she knew to keep the child spirit away. She had taken to eating hot peppers and burning herbs. She had lost trust in The Dark One and the Voodoo conjures seemed to work; for a while.

Saturday night was always a busy time for both witches and Voodoo followers. Christelle's windows were opened due to the heat. She saw a shadow walk past late in the night. She closed her eyes and followed it with her mind. The passerby was not familiar. He was a dark, skinny man. He was a seer.

New Orleans knew of, and was even secretly proud of its Voodoo, but having a witch in the city was different. Witchcraft was associated with conjuring Satan. Maurie Laveau and her followers were members of the holy church and believers in Jesus Christ. Their traditions they practiced had been passed down for centuries to cast goodness and help others with sickness and heartaches.

Witchcraft was evil and could not be allowed to be practiced anywhere. Witches were the Devil's helpers and they had to be hunted and destroyed.

Seers were rare. They didn't reveal their talents for fear of being thought a witch. They were enemies of witches because they could find them and reveal them, but witches could do the same. Seers were also not affected by most spells of voodoo or common witchcraft, but the Dark One had the power to make the seer's mind hazy and confuse them with their magic. It became a match of wit, strength, and power; a circle of torment and inevitable destruction.

His name was Titus. He had lived for hundreds of years and had seen more than most. He wasn't a demon, or an angel. His purpose was to keep a balance between good and evil. For centuries he had hunted demons and witches, but his own identity had to be kept secret. Being in New Orleans at this time was the most dangerous thing Titus had done thus far. In such a small area he had found a Mambo voodoo princess, a demon, and a coven of witches. He knew that he was walking a fine line that could destroy him and his lineage of seers.

This triangle of magic was feared by Titus, but he was drawn to New Orleans by Lisette. She needed his help to move on. Battling the witches would be hard, but the Dark One would be even more difficult. Titus had followed Lisette in the distance. He knew she was frightened and did not want to scare her away. Maurie could retrieve her soul, but it would not be easy.

Lisette Lefevre came from a long line of ancestors deep in the French lineage of the Descoteaux's family. Her great-great-grandmother had been a seer. She had lived an unusual short life of only a half century due to an untimely account with Azazel's first Magni, Genevieve Deloflota.

Angelique Descoteaux was a beautiful woman. She had only known of her power of seeing for a decennial. She was new at her craft, and became obsessed with unveiling the identity of Genevieve as a witch. In her haste and inexperience, she was no match for Genevieve and Azazel. Her body was found hung and burned from a tree deep in the Forêt de Loches. She left three children; none of them were ever identified as a seer.

Lisette's mother was a devout Catholic. She would lock herself in her room for days. Her husband and children had no idea what possessed her at these times. She feared her power to be the work of Satan. When visions would come to her, she would hide and pray for them to go away. She didn't know how to control them. She would scream and fast until she would pass out. But even in her sleep these visions would haunt her.

When Lisette was five, she became very sick. Her fever would not break and Father Antonio was called to the home. When he arrived on the doorstep with Maurie Laveau, Lisette's mother did not want Satan to enter her home, but she trusted Father Antonio. She was distraught when Lisette lost her battle. The father blessed the child's body as Maurie held Lisette's tormented mother in her arms. Two days after her daughter's death, Lisette's mother took her own life. Now she was damned to spend eternity with the one she had feared the most in life. Lisette's lost spirit had no idea her mother had passed on.

Lisette roamed the streets of New Orleans looking for her family. Her father had taken her brother and sister back to France after his wife's suicide. She had no idea that she had been lost for sixteen years. Time is different when you are dead. She was still a five-year-old child. With the help of Maurie's spells and Titus' visions, Lisette had managed to stay invisible to the Dark One. Christelle had no awareness of Lisette, or of her soul that was trapped inside her. Lisette knew Christelle was not a good person. She was dark and cold; no warmth radiated from her. But there was a small tug somewhere that kept Lisette coming back to her.

Chapter Ten

The smell of fresh croissants and delectable pastries mingled with the unbelievably wonderful smell of fresh breads. The French Bakery on Saint Charles was one of New Orleans's favorite bakeries. Aimeri Cheuvront could not keep his wares on the shelves. He knew most of his success was due to what happened in the back room of his bakery; not the kitchen, but the room beyond.

The small building that now housed the bakery was not very old. It had been built ten years ago on a site of history that not too many people were aware of in New Orleans. This particular corner of Saint Charles Street was the spot where the first person was hung for witchcraft during the vigilante movement in New Orleans. A man, name unknown, had been accused of witchcraft and was strung up from a craggy, old tree whose roots were still alive under the ground below the building.

It was said he had saluted the small crowd just before the rope snapped his neck. After he was pronounced dead, his body was burned right on the rope; his ashes piling up on the ground below. The story goes that a wind was stirring yet the ashes were not blown, but were sucked into the ground leaving a dead spot. No grass would grow, not even a weed in the area where the witch's ashes had landed.

When Aimeri opened The French Bakery it only took a few days for him to realize bread and pastries were not the only things that were being made there. The landlord had given him keys to the front door only. He had use of the front showroom and the small kitchen along with a stockroom and a small office upstairs. At the back of the kitchen was another door which remained locked. The landlord had told him it was for his own personal storage, and he would use the back door if he needed entrance.

Curiosity had gotten Aimeri one evening, and he had walked to the back door to shake the doorknob. He put his ear to the door and could hear hushed voices. There was no one in the bakery. Shaking the doorknob harder, he was shocked when the door came opened. The room was dark and no voices could be heard. Aimeri stepped inside just enough to see the only thing in the room was a stairway leading down. His eyes played tricks on him, and shadows seemed to glide across the walls of the room. From the bottom of the stairway a whisper came. It called his name. He shut the door and never tried it again. Aimeri was a good Catholic man, but he was also a believer in the darker spirits that lived in New Orleans. Whatever happened in that back room was not of his concern.

❦

The Murder flew to the back of the bakery. The door was already opened, and the four hags were no more than shadows as they entered it and shut the door behind them. Christelle and the Dark One were already there. Candles lit the walls of the room below. The wall on the right had another entry with no door. The darkness that crept through the hole was thick. No candle light could penetrate it.

Another presence was there, but it was not detected. It stayed in the shadows of the far corner, invisible to all present. Titus was not far away. He was watching, and could also "see" the tiny spirit of Lisette hiding in the corner. Maurie was at her home on Saint Anne's, sitting in the back room with her eyes closed and her mind straining to hear the conjure of the five witches and the demon. She didn't know Lisette was also there, but she felt she was near.

All of this activity concentrated in one small area caused light from the moon to slowly wane, yet there wasn't a cloud in the sky. A streak of lightning ran across the Crescent City, and a crack of thunder rolled from one corner to the other. Maurie opened her eyes, and the seer moved on his way. The witches dropped each other's hands and all looked at the Dark One. His eyes remained closed, but the slight crease on his forehead told them he was aware of the disturbance. Lisette remained quiet in the corner, and smiled at the trouble she had just caused.

PART II

Chapter Eleven

Titus had finally met with Maurie. They both knew they needed to work together, and the decision was made to get Christelle that night. Lisette was still a child, but becoming more powerful without knowing it. Her mother's power as a seer was transferred to her. Lisette knew she was drawn to Christelle for a reason, but her visions had not yet shown her why.

The sky was bubbling with black clouds, while the wind was too still to be believed. New Orleans had seen its share of storms, and this one was going to be a big one.

Before the sky spilled its fury, the crows needed to get to low ground. The best place for them was the back room of the bakery.

This was exactly what Maurie needed. It had to distract the hags enough to make them leave Christelle's residence. No warning of the mob could be given to Christelle. Maurie counted on perfect timing.

Maurie prayed to Mawu for help to contact the child spirit and gain trust. Mawu listened, and opened Lisette's eyes. He guided her to Maurie and now the three of them knew what to do.

Azazel felt Lisette's power, and he knew Maurie was involved. He felt a seer was also close. Knowing this dulled his focus. Christelle was not important enough to fight them all. The coven of hags was old and useless to him. His decision to leave New Orleans was made.

Maurie and Titus felt his withdrawal. They had to retrieve Christelle in order for Lisette's journey to be completed. The Dark One would be back to carry out his revenge, and that would be their true battle.

∞

Maurie guided the mob down the narrow cobblestone streets. They were going to rid their town of a witch! They had been warned of Christelle's powers. Maurie had instructed the men that she had to be taken quickly, and with no harm to her.

"You must bind her hands and feet quickly to keep her from conjuring. Her mouth must be bound. Make sure no one makes direct eye contact with her."

Maurie would need to work fast to muddle her senses and lessen her powers. Once the spell of capture had been completed, she would no longer be a threat. Titus was sure he had seen success, though he had warned of some problems and could not see to the end.

The men were restless. Maurie could see the fear in their faces. Even her Voodoo couldn't guarantee them safety.

Maurie spoke to the mob as lightning streaked the sky and the wind began to whip around the corners of the buildings.

"Four men will enter the front and two from the back. Christelle will be awake, but her attention will be on something else. You must quickly capture her and bind her tight. Make sure to put the gag in her mouth and do not look into her eyes. She is very strong; you must not let her small frame deceive you. No harm can come to her. Cover her eyes with this cloth. I will then begin the spell of capture. You must hold her down so I can place the candles around her body. Since you will be in the circle, you may feel strange things, but fear not. Do not take your concentration off of holding her down. Enter when you see me at Christelle's window."

Maurie left the men a few houses down from Christelle's residence. She walked into the night by herself; the men could not see the small child spirit beside her.

As they reached the front, Maurie bent down and looked into Lisette's eyes. They had already discussed what she must do. Lisette was still fearful of Christelle, but she knew she must do this to retrieve her soul. Her mother was waiting for her.

⁂

Christelle tossed in a fitful sleep as the thunder signaled danger in the storm. She heard a sigh just a few feet from the foot of her bed. Sitting up, a translucent figure of a child appeared. It was the damned spirit that had haunted her a few nights before.

A flicker of movement by the window caught her attention. Standing there was Maurie Laveau. The shock of seeing the spirit and Maurie, together in her bedroom, paralyzed her for just a second. Suddenly, a commotion came busting through her door. Several men forced her back onto her bed. Two on her left and two on her right, they began tying her hands and feet together. One stood at the head of the bed with a cloth in his hands. Christelle shot fire from her eyes and screamed a blood-curdling scream. The man with the blindfold fell to his knees holding his head. Blood was pouring from his eyes, nose, mouth and ears.

Maurie grabbed the cloth herself and tied it over Christelle's eyes. She fought like a tiger. One of the bindings came loose and she struck out with her left foot, hitting something solid and heard bone crack. Christelle was screaming incomprehensible words as Maurie fought to get the gag in her mouth before any more incantations came spewing out. Another man dropped to the floor – out cold. The storm began to whip into a frenzy outside. Christelle's shutters pounded against the glass; windows broke and rain began to shoot through. Lisette began to cry.

Maurie could not comfort her, but yelled over the wind and rain, "Sweet one, Lisette, be strong. Do not falter. This is all for you."

The remaining four men picked the thrashing Christelle up off the bed and placed her on the bedroom floor with a thud, holding her down the best they could. Maurie pulled the candles from her robe, but knew the whipping wind coming through the broken windows would not allow her to light them. They had to get her someplace where the candles could be lit.

"Take her downstairs to the parlor."

Christelle continued to fight with the strength of a man as they struggled to bring her down the stairs. Half way down, the men lost their hold. She slid down the remaining stairs, but her bindings held. She was still. They hurriedly drug her to the middle of the parlor floor. Maurie began to place the candles in a circle around her now still body.

The spell of capture was completed. Christelle was now being controlled by Maurie. Holding Lisette in her arms, she whispered in her ear, "Mon Cher, you will be in your mother's arms very soon." Lisette was silent; her slight form shook with fear.

Titus appeared and shouted over the storm, "Ms. Laveau, we must leave. The storm is gaining strength, and I have seen danger coming near."

Chapter Twelve

Maurie tended to the two men that had gone down during the capture. One had a broken jaw from the kick Christelle had sent. The other man was gone. He had unfortunately looked into her eyes and lost his life in the fight. Maurie would have his body retrieved after the storm.

Christelle was still out. They had no choice but to carry her through the storm to Maurie's home. They wrapped her up in a sheet like a mummy. The four men grabbed the four corners and rushed out into the fury. Maurie comforted Lisette the best she could and hid her under the many folds in her heavy robe. They both stepped out into the street that immediately lit up with a cragged bolt of thick lightning. The thunder was tremendous. Maurie's home was several blocks away. Titus rushed behind them, trying to hurry up their steps, and helping the hurt man through the wet streets. He feared what he had seen in his vision, but had not shared it with Maurie.

Just as the strange group of capturers reached Maurie's gate, the rain stopped. A few more bolts of lightning flitted across the sky, and it was over. The storm had lasted just long enough to cover their deed. Maurie knew the hags would be out soon, and it wouldn't take them long to discover what had taken place at Christelle's residence. She quickly conjured a spell of protection that would hold them at bay for a while. She ordered the men to place Christelle in the back room and to tie her down. They left by the back door, thankful that this deed was done. Maurie made a poultice for the injured man's jaw and sent him home.

Titus sat in the kitchen with Lisette. He was soaked to the skin, yet she was not even damp. The fire roared in the fireplace as Titus shivered and tried to warm himself. Maurie fixed him a cup of steaming hot tea. They were not finished yet.

An ear-splitting rumble shattered the silence in the kitchen. It came from the back room. Maurie looked at Titus and could see the fear on his face. All three felt the evil presence before they ever laid eyes on him. Azazel was back. Maurie's only concern at the moment was to protect Lisette. Titus knew he had to face him, because either way he was going to have to fight. He rushed to the door all the while praying silently to Mawu for protection against the darkness in the next room. He fully expected to see Christelle untied, but she remained bound.

Maurie entered behind Titus, also shocked to see Christelle still bound and gagged on the floor. Only her blindfold had been removed, as if the Dark One wanted her to witness his power. Christelle's eyes looked questioning upon Azazel.

"I did not come back for you, Rita. You are weak and selfish. I am only here to inflict my revenge on these two meddling simple magicians and retrieve the child's soul which I should never have allowed to be housed in your body of filth."

The Dark One eyed Titus. Without saying anything, he began to send vicious and violent visions to him of the past two hundred years of his evil deeds. Titus was paralyzed as his mind held him in terrifying fear.

He then turned to hold Maurie's gaze. She showed no fear as she held tight to Lisette behind her. He hurled a spear of fire towards her, but it seemed to hit an invisible wall just inches from her and fell to the floor. The fire circled Maurie and Lisette, but did not touch them.

Christelle looked at Maurie with a new awareness. Suddenly, the wall of fire circling them went out. Maurie felt Christelle's powers. She was giving them to Maurie to use, leaving herself defenseless against Azazel.

Christelle then noticed the small spirit. Lisette was sending visions of the night her mother had given birth to her. She heard the screams of pain and terror waft through the swamp. She saw the Murder of crows circling the hut, and the Dark One taking the baby, her, from the young black girl. She watched the conjuring of the spirit's soul and saw it enter into her own. It had been with her all her life. This little spirit had not meant to do anything but retrieve her soul. Christelle felt something tugging, trying to leave. She knew the spirit was going home. Then she felt as if huge hands were squeezing her lungs, heart, and brain as if she was being squished just like the egg she had crushed in her hands.

Maurie closed her eyes. All she could do was battle the orb of evil that filled the room with her energy and the powers Christelle had given her. The room began to hum. Suddenly, Titus was freed from his visions. Lisette walked slowly to Maurie and took her hand. The three of them stood silently, concentrating together on the evilness in the room. The noise grew louder, as if electricity was surging from the walls.

The room exploded with light then dark. The noise was unbearable, then sucked into the darkness, leaving only the silence. Maurie felt both her hands being squeezed tightly; one by an old leathery hand with long, bony fingers, and the other with a small, trembling hand of a child.

As if opening her eyes, the light in the room began to escape from the shadows. Maurie, Titus, and Lisette stood alone. Christelle and Azazel had vanished. Only Christelle's bindings lay on the ground, still in tight knots.

Maurie stooped down and took Lisette's small face into her hands. The child smiled and whispered, "Thank you." Then she extended her hand to an unseen figure in the room and slowly disappeared. Maurie knew she was going home. Tears rolled down her cheeks as she turned to Titus. He shook his head as if confirming Maurie's thoughts. Moonbeams shone through the window and onto the floor where Christelle had been lying just moments before. Maurie and Titus both knew that Mawu had been there with them. She was now guiding Lisette back to her mother. The question on both their lips was where was Christelle? Had she been taken by Azazel? Or had Mawu sent her away to safety?

Maurie hurried over to the table and lit three candles of peace. Titus swept the floor and laid a fresh line of brick-dust on the back threshold. Echoes of conjures were heard throughout the night, sending thanks to Mawu and peace to everyone that had been touched by the activities of the night. They both kept the corner of their eyes searching for shadows of Azazel. He would be back – over and over again.

Chapter Thirteen

The storm had caused damage throughout the city. Trees were toppled, and roofs had been torn off houses as if they were paper in a child's hands. But the next morning brought bright sunshine and a cleansing breeze.

Maurie had not slept at all. Her thoughts had been jumbled with both evil and goodness. Her fears crept around during the night, keeping her eyes open.

As she walked out into the morning shine, she was aware of a beautiful bluebird sitting on her gate post. The bird was looking at her. Maurie stared back at the bird, and then watched as it soared and circled above three times before flying east. Maurie knew Christelle was safe and the evil that once was contained inside her was gone. Mawu had blessed them many times last night.

Maurie continued her journey to the church. She wanted blessings from Father Antonio. Afterwards, she would go visit the home of the man that was killed last night. Titus had fetched his body and taken it home, telling his wife that he had found him under a tree right after the storm had subsided. Maurie's heart was heavy for his family. She had said prayers and incantations to soothe their pain.

Titus had moved on to find others that needed his specialties. Staying apart would help protect them both.

Maurie fingered the amulet and the small cross that she wore around her neck. Both powers had saved her life, and sent a tiny angel home. Were they enough to keep her safe from the evil out there?

As she entered the huge, wooden doors of St. Louis, the glows of hundreds of candles lit her soul. She felt uplifted and safe within these walls. Father Antonio looked up and smiled when he saw her entering the sanctuary. He had just lit a candle, one from the section for children.

Chapter Fourteen

Present Day - New Orleans, LA

The streets of the city are bustling with people from all over the world. It smells of stale beer, spicy food, sweat, and sex. It has become a place for young people to carouse the streets of the quarter for cheap drinks and naked women. But in the back streets, the times have not changed the old city much.

The tomb of Maurie Laveau can be found at St. Louis Cemetery #1 on Rampart Street. It is covered with X's and gifts are left on a daily basis. But the real mystery is which tomb really holds Maurie's body. A white crypt with the name of the Glapion family, and a small plaque that states it is Maurie's resting place as well, is the most common place for tourists to visit to pay their respects.

The dispute is created by an unmarked crypt in the back of the cemetery where many people believe to be Maurie's true resting place. Both are marked with X's and piled high with cigarettes, booze, lipstick, money, candy, and other gifts that people leave for good luck. This back tomb even has a set of keys mortared into the bricks of the reddish crypt. The belief in voodoo is still prominent and represented daily at both crypts at Saint Louis Cemetery #1.

Many rumors have circulated of people seeing Maurie's spirit roaming the cemetery, sometimes with her white snake, Zombie. Others have reported of a black cat that is believed to be another form Maurie takes. Another famous spirit that occupies the cemetery is Alphonse. He is reported to take your hand and ask you to find his home. Saint Louis Cemetery is both eerie and beautiful in a spiritual sense. It is said you should walk out of the cemetery backwards to prevent taking a spirit with you.

Ghosts and Voodoo are not just confined to the cement walls of the cemeteries of New Orleans. Ask any restaurant, hotel, or bar owner if their building is haunted, and the answer will be a resounding – Yes!

Thais Solano, owner of the Pirate's Alley Café, located in a small, historical alley beside Saint Louis Cathedral, knows of many spirits that haunt the quarter and refuse to hide. She tells of some, and keeps others to herself. Jean Lafitte, himself, was jailed in the building where the Pirate Bar is now. The grounds are hallowed with historical events of murderous duels, evil treachery, and dirty dealings between politicians, pirates, and privateers. The famous absinthe is also served here using the antique glass dripping fountain to drip the ice cold water over the cube of sugar balancing on the absinthe spoon. Absinthe is also known as the "Green Fairy." The use of wormwood in the liquor was known for causing hallucinations, but in witchcraft it is used to conjure the spirits of the dead. Is this a coincidence?

Dr. John can be found seven days a week at the Voodoo Museum, also located on a small cross street between Bourbon and Royal. It is dedicated mostly to Maurie and her work as a volunteer nurse and outstanding citizen of New Orleans. Her death certificate is displayed on the wall, along with many articles of her dedication to the people of the city. Dr. John is a Voodoo priest, son of a Voodoo queen. His piercing, pale blue eyes grab hold of you as you enter the small room where he presides over his inheritance. He once told me he could see my dreams, and I believe him. Here you can purchase spiritual candles, Voodoo dolls, and gris-gris bags for almost any reason or occasion. He always seems to know what you are looking for before you tell him. He will also give you a reading if you dare.

Above the museum live seven snakes, mostly pythons, including an albino python, and a black mamba. The pythons slither free at all times, but the deadly mamba is kept in a cage. Dr. John owns total respect from his pythons mainly because they know he is one of them.

The gist of Voodoo in New Orleans boils down to this; the creator-god is very distant and doesn't involve himself with us. But spiritual entities stand between us and God and they love to manipulate our world. They appreciate being worshipped and asked for help. And millions of people each year ask, and many are rewarded; be it Voodoo or just coincidence.

Through the neighborhoods of Louisiana, Voodoo and witchcraft are still very prevalent. Its spirit is felt as you walk through the quarter. Every night tourists are seen walking with others in ghost tours, and Voodoo and witchcraft stores line the streets around it.

Whether they believe it or not, the people of today know of Voodoo. When someone becomes sick, whispers of that person being "fixed" can be heard. More often than not, prayers are not the only things being sent asking for good health. Herbs and incense are used, along with incantations, candles, and gris-gris bags.

New Orleans is a town that never sleeps. Every morning, the revelry of the night before is washed from the streets, but its secrets remain. The spirits retreat; awaiting another moon. Rest comes with heavy rains and unrelenting heat. But the night is for magic.

Made in the USA
Middletown, DE
17 January 2019